# SEA PATROL TO THE RESCUE!

**Based on the episode "Pups Save a Baby Octopus" by James Backshall and Jeff Sweeney**

**Illustrated by Nate Lovett**

**A Random House PICTUREBACK® Book**

Random House  New York

rhcbooks.com

ISBN 978-1-5247-6875-1

Printed in the United States of America

10 9 8 7 6 5 4

One sunny morning, the PAW Patrol were at their new Beach Tower headquarters. Mayor Goodway had asked the pups to be Adventure Beach's new lifeguard rescue team. She wanted them on duty during her luau that afternoon.

"We'll be the Sea Patrol," Ryder announced. "But before you can save anyone, you'll have to earn your lifeguard badges."

"Ready, set, get wet!" barked Zuma.

For the lifeguard test, the pups didn't rescue a person. They took turns swimming through a course of floating buoys and rescuing a pineapple named Mr. Prickly! One by one, each pup earned a badge . . . until it was Rocky's turn.

"That's okay," he said. "I don't like getting wet."

"You can't be a lifeguard without getting wet," Skye said.

"Hmmm," Rocky said to himself. "We'll see about that!"

Instead of swimming, Rocky jumped from buoy to buoy, then threw a life ring around Mr. Prickly. He pulled the pineapple in and hopped back to shore without getting wet!

"Cool rescue technique," Ryder said. "But if you want to earn your lifeguard badge, you have to swim."

Rocky was happy to be a land guard.

"I know you can do this," said Ryder. "If you don't feel up to it now, you can try again later."

Meanwhile, Cap'n Turbot was out at sea feeding Wally the Walrus. "Here's some more juicy jellyfish jerky," he said. He didn't realize that a baby octopus was stuck to the side of his chum bucket.

Suddenly, the water started churning, and Cap'n Turbot's boat, the *Flounder,* began to rock. Giant tentacles reached out of the waves and wrapped around the boat.

"Great gushing geysers—I need the PAW Patrol!" Cap'n Turbot exclaimed, and he called Ryder.

Ryder told the pups about Cap'n Turbot's boat. "The Sea Patrol is on a roll!"

"Um, Ryder, how are we going to get out to the *Flounder*?" Rubble asked.

Ryder pushed a button on his PupPad.

The Beach Tower shook as a huge ship called the *Sea Patroller* detached from it. Robo Dog was at the controls, and he loaded Zuma's and Rubble's special sea vehicles onto it.

Ryder, Rubble, Zuma, and Marshall hopped aboard, and the *Sea Patroller* sped to the rescue.

The *Sea Patroller* reached the troubled *Flounder*. Zuma and Rubble hit the waves in their new sea vehicles.

Zuma tried to pull the tentacles off Cap'n Turbot's boat with his vehicle's mechanical arms, but the sea monster was too strong.

Ryder had an idea. He told Robo Dog to sound the *Sea Patroller*'s horn.
*BWAAAAAAAA!*
The startled sea monster released the *Flounder* and slid back below the ocean's surface.
"Hooray!" everyone cheered.
But just then, the *Flounder* started to sink— and Cap'n Turbot was still on it!

Rubble used his crane to pluck Cap'n Turbot off the deck—just as the boat slipped under the waves.

"The pups and I will do everything we can to raise the *Flounder*," Ryder promised.

As Rubble headed back to land, no one noticed the little stowaway stuck to Cap'n Turbot's life ring.

Marshall put on his scuba gear, dove into the water, and went to work. He found the sunken *Flounder* and started pumping it full of air from his tanks. The boat floated up toward the surface.

As Marshall watched the boat rise, something shiny caught his eye. Was it undersea treasure?

He picked it up with his mechanical claw and shook it. "It's a baby rattle!" he exclaimed.

Meanwhile, Cap'n Turbot was back on Adventure Beach trying to cheer himself up at Mayor Goodway's luau. But while he looked for something to eat, the baby octopus jumped off him and landed on Mayor Humdinger's head!

"Help!" the mayor shouted. "Get it off!"

Just then, the sea monster rose out of the waves! Skye took to the air with her parasail to distract it while Rubble built a sand wall to protect the beachgoers.

When Ryder arrived, he saw that the sea monster was actually an octopus—and it was squinting. "It's looking for something, but it can't see very well."

"Well, keep it away from me," muttered Mayor Humdinger. "I don't want that on my head, too!"

Then Ryder realized the giant octopus was the little octopus's mother. "We need to get that baby back to its mom!"

But first they had to get the baby off Mayor Humdinger's head. Marshall remembered the rattle he'd found and started shaking it.

The baby octopus reached for the toy . . . but because Mayor Humdinger couldn't see, he accidentally knocked the rattle into the ocean!

Someone had to get that rattle!

"I can find it with my metal detector," said Rocky.

"Are you sure, Rocky?" Ryder asked. "You'll have to swim and get wet."

"If getting wet will help the baby octopus get back to its mom, I can do it!" Rocky declared. He extended his metal detector, bravely dove into the water, and found the rattle!

Shaking the toy, Zuma boarded the *Sea Patroller* with Ryder and headed away from the beach. The little octopus followed the rattling noise . . . and the mother followed her baby. Out in the deep water, the mother and baby found each other and hugged.

Ryder quickly made eyeglasses out of two punch bowls from the luau. Now the mother could always find her baby. The Sea Patrol had worked together and saved the day!

Back on the beach, everyone cheered for the pups—and for Cap'n Turbot's newly repaired *Flounder*.

"Thank you, PAW Patrol," said Mayor Goodway. "You saved the beach *and* the party!"

"I think Rocky deserves the biggest thank-you," said Ryder. "He got wet to save the day and earned this." Ryder pinned a lifeguard badge to Rocky's vest. All the pups howled and hoorayed for their brave friend!